ON A TRAIN FULL OF DYNAMITE!

"Don't worry about me," Remy calls back. "I'll time it perfectly."

The locomotive rumbles along, pushing the flatcar with Remy and the dynamite in front of it. José gallops ahead at top speed, passing the train. He is almost to the switch that will send it hurtling toward the wall when he cries out and slumps across the saddle.

"Oh, no! José has been hit!" you cry out. You realize you're going to have to take care of the switch yourself.

You and your horse fly ahead like the wind. You pass the train and reach the switch with seconds to spare. Still mounted, you swing down from the saddle and grab the lever, pulling it forward.

The train lurches onto the spur line and speeds toward a wooden barrier. Remy lights the short fuse on the dynamite and jumps clear. Ten seconds later, the train reaches the barrier, smashes through, and hurtles toward the wall. The shock wave from the explosion behind you nearly knocks you out of the saddle.

As you ride off, artillery shells whistle out of the sky and start to explode around you. What will you do?

ONLY YOU, AS YOUNG INDIANA JONES, CAN DECIDE. . . .

THE YOUNG INDIANA JONES CHRONICLES™

Book 2
SOUTH OF THE BORDER

MEXICO, March 1916

By Richard Brightfield

Adapted from the television movie
"Young Indiana Jones and the Curse of
the Jackal"
Teleplay by Jonathan Hales
Story by George Lucas

Illustrated by Frank Bolle

BANTAM BOOKS
NEW YORK · TORONTO · LONDON · SYDNEY · AUCKLAND

RL 5, age 10 and up

SOUTH OF THE BORDER
A Bantam Book / July 1992

*CHOOSE YOUR OWN ADVENTURE® is a registered trademark of
Bantam Books, a division of Bantam Doubleday
Dell Publishing Group, Inc.
Registered in U.S. Patent and Trademark Office and elsewhere.
Original conception of Edward Packard*

*THE YOUNG INDIANA JONES CHRONICLES℗
is a trademark of Lucasfilm Ltd.
All rights reserved. Used under authorization.*

*Cover art by George Tsui
Interior illustrations by Frank Bolle*

ISBN 0-553-29757-0

Published simultaneously in the United States and Canada

Bantam Books are published by Bantam Books, a division of Bantam Doubleday Dell Publishing Group, Inc. Its trademark, consisting of the words "Bantam Books" and the portrayal of a rooster, is Registered in U.S. Patent and Trademark Office and in other countries. Marca Registrada. Bantam Books, 666 Fifth Avenue, New York, New York 10103.

PRINTED IN THE UNITED STATES OF AMERICA

OPM   0 9 8 7 6 5 4 3

SOUTH OF
THE BORDER

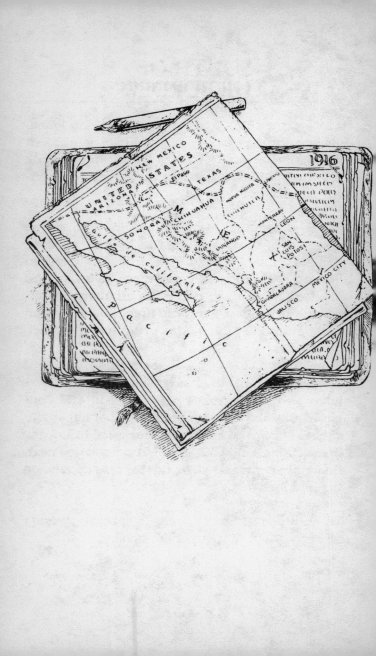

Your Adventure

The year is 1916. You are young Indiana Jones, the son of a professor of medieval studies at Princeton University in New Jersey. In this book you are traveling through Mexico with your cousin Frank.

In the adventures that follow, you will get to meet many famous figures in history, such as Pancho Villa, General Pershing, and General Patton. You will also experience life during the Mexican Revolution, and learn all about the latest military advances of the time. You may even get a firsthand look at the corruption of power!

From time to time as you read along, you will be asked to make a choice. The adventures you have as Indiana Jones are the results of your choices. You are responsible because you choose. After you make your decision, follow the instructions to find out what happens to you next. Remember, your Mexican adventures depend on the actions you decide to take.

To help you in your travels, a special glossary is provided at the end of the book.

Chronology

1521 The native Aztec empire is overthrown by forces under the command of the Spanish adventurer, Hernán Cortés.

1521–1821 Mexico is a Spanish colony.

1821 Revolt led by Augustin de Iturbide forces Spain to recognize Mexican independence.

1845 The United States annexes Texas, which had declared its independence from Mexico a decade earlier.

1846–1848 War with the United States strips Mexico of its northwestern provinces, including New Mexico and northern California.

1857 Benito Juárez becomes president.

1864 French forces occupy Mexico on inability of Mexico to pay its debts. The French set up the Austrian archduke Maximilian as emperor.

1867 The French withdraw their troops on the demand of the U.S. under the "Monroe Doctrine." Maximilian executed by the Mexicans.

1876 Porfirio Díaz seizes power.

1910–1911 Francisco Madero organizes effective revolt against Díaz and is elected president.

1913 Victoriana Huerta, Madero's military commander, has Madero murdered and seizes power. Pancho Villa and Zapata organize revolts against his rule.

1914 Venustiano Carranza ousts Huerta and becomes president.

1915–1916 Civil war in which the forces of Carranza defeat both Villa and Zapata.

You are Indiana Jones. You were born in July 1899 in Princeton, New Jersey, where your father is a professor of medieval studies at the university. It is now 1916, and you are sixteen years old.

You are hitchhiking along a desert road in New Mexico with your cousin Frank. He is two years older than you—tall and lanky with a shock of dark hair hanging over his forehead. It is late afternoon, but the sun is still bright and very hot. Your face is shaded by the broad rim of your favorite hat, and the strap of a leather satchel is slung over your shoulder.

At the moment, you and Frank are walking south, occasionally looking back over your shoulders to scan the road for a possible lift.

Finally you hear the sound of a vehicle in the distance, chugging in your direction from the north. As it gets closer, you see that it's an old Model T pickup truck. You stick out your thumb hopefully.

The pickup slows a bit but sails right past the two of you, kicking up a cloud of dust in your faces.

$\rightarrow$ $\rightarrow$ $\rightarrow$ $\rightarrow$ $\rightarrow$ $\rightarrow$ $\rightarrow$ $\rightarrow$ $\rightarrow$ $\rightarrow$ $\rightarrow$ $\rightarrow$ $\rightarrow$

Turn to page 2.

"Darn!" you say.

"Just our luck. Stuck out here in the middle of nowhere and—" Frank starts.

"Hey, wait a minute," you interrupt. "It looks like it's stopping."

A few hundred feet past you, the truck comes to a stop with a screech of its brakes. You and Frank dash down the road. A gray-bearded farmer is driving.

"Can you give us a ride, mister?" you say through the side window.

"Reckon I will. Yank real hard on that door, and jump in. Whereabouts ya goin'?" the farmer asks, as he starts off down the road.

"It's our spring break from school. We thought we'd hitch to Mexico—have a little fun."

"Well, not much fun goin' on down there right now," the farmer says, "what with all them tinhorn dictators fightin' each other and shootin' up the countryside."

"Well, I thought we'd just take a look and—" you start.

"Only goin' to a few miles this side of Columbus," the farmer puts in. "You'll have to walk or get another ride from there."

"That's fine with us," Frank says. "Is Columbus close to the border?"

"Pretty close."

You watch the sun set over the distant mountains to the west—a gleaming red ball falling out of an orange-colored sky. After that, you ride for hours on a straight road that seems to stretch endlessly into the darkness. The headlights of the truck keep a constant puddle of dim light in front of you.

You and Frank doze as the farmer drives relentlessly through the night.

Finally the headlights illuminate a faded sign that reads COLUMBUS 5 MILES.

"This is as far as I go in this direction," the farmer says, elbowing you awake.

"Thanks, mister," you say, climbing out of the truck.

"Thanks again," Frank says.

"You're welcome," the farmer says with a wave.

The truck chugs off, turning onto a side road. You and Frank watch as its taillights, like two red eyes, cross the desert, then disappear far away.

"My watch said 4:00 A.M. while I could still see it," Frank says.

"We might as well keep going and stay warm walking," you say. "It's gotten a bit chilly."

"You're right," Frank says. "I don't feel like sleeping on the ground tonight, anyway."

→ → → → → → → → → → → →

Go on to the next page.

* * *

A couple of hours later, in the first gray light of dawn, you and Frank see the dim outline of a town up ahead. You cross a single line of railroad tracks, pass a small wooden station, and walk into Columbus.

There's a two-story hotel with a narrow porch in front and a one-story general store. A tiny dress shop is squeezed in between. Most of the buildings are made of adobe—bricks of plastered sun-dried earth—and have seen better days. On the other side of the street are a stable, a blacksmith's shop, and a few residences. Up at the far end is the one-story bank built of real brick, the only building in town not made of wood or adobe. It has a somewhat fancy entrance made of carved limestone, with two "Greek" columns and triangular ornamentation framing the doorway.

A few scraps of tumbleweed blow across the road as you head up toward it.

"Guess nobody's up at this hour," Frank says.

"I think there's someone in front of the bank," you say. "It looks like a soldier."

"A soldier?" Frank asks.

Sure enough, a grizzled-looking soldier, with a face like tanned leather, is leaning half asleep against one of the pillars.

"Hello," you say.

→ → → → → → → → → → → → →

Go on to the next page.

The soldier looks up, shaking his head to get the cobwebs out. "You two are up kinda early," he says with a gravelly voice.

"Is there someplace around here where we can get something to eat?" you ask.

"Sure thing," he says. "Try the hotel over 'cross the street in about an hour. There's a dinin' room off the lobby. Just ask for—"

Suddenly a shot rings out.

The sentry staggers backward, dropping his rifle and clutching his chest, where a red stain is rapidly spreading. He slumps to his knees as his eyes glaze over, then topples to the ground.

Another shot, and a bullet pings off the side of the doorway not far from your head.

"Somebody's shooting at us," Frank says. "We'd better get away from here—quick!"

Both of you start running as more shots ring out.

You glance back and see where the bullets are coming from. A line of horsemen is charging into town behind you. They look like pictures you've seen of Mexican bandits, wearing high sombreros with huge upturned brims and cartridge belts of bullets crisscrossing their chests.

→ → → → → → → → → → → →

Go on to the next page.

You realize that you have only seconds to get off the street. On your left, a short way down, is a narrow walkway between the stable and the forge. Close by on the right, there's a large wood-pile next to the hotel porch, near the front of the dress shop.

→ → → → → → → → → → → →

If you make a dash for the walkway,
turn to page 57.
If you try for the woodpile, turn to page 22.

You decide to stay in the wagon for the time being. For the rest of the night it bounces along, and by dawn it comes to a stop. A short time later, Remy pulls up the back flap of your wagon and looks in.

"You are still here, I see," he says, surprised. "How about some chow and coffee?"

The wagons are in a "pioneer" circle with a campfire already blazing in the center. You get out and follow Remy over to it. Nearby a row of women are pounding on broad, flat stones with other stones that look like rolling pins.

Remy notices you gazing at them. "They are grinding corn on *metates* with *metlapils*," he says. "Soon we will have some fine tortillas. In the meantime, try this."

He hands you a battered tin cup filled with coffee. It's very thick, black, and—as you soon discover—the grounds are still on the bottom. It reminds you of the Turkish coffee you tasted in Egypt.

The coffee wakes you up a bit. You stretch and look out around the campfire. You see two men standing next to the fire, talking to Villa and Cardenas. One of them has an artificial hand— in the shape of a pair of shears.

→ → → → → → → → → → → →

Turn to page 24.

"Vamos, caballeros!—Let's go, horsemen!" one of them shouts, as he leaps onto his horse. He gallops out of town with the others following, firing departing shots into the now-flaming buildings.

You and Frank wait another couple of minutes, then cautiously stand up and look around. Flaming embers are beginning to fall all around from the building behind you.

"Look out!" Frank says, pulling you back down. A lone straggler is galloping up the street. He reigns in his horse in front of the dress shop, its glass display window shattered but otherwise miraculously unscathed. The horseman reaches into the window and grabs a couple of the dresses.

At the same moment, an attractive young woman comes running out. "Give me back my dresses!" she shouts. The horse whirls around, knocking the woman to the ground. She sits there, shaking her fist, as the horseman gallops away.

At that moment, a riderless horse comes trotting down the street.

"I'll get your dresses back for you, ma'am," you call over to the woman, as you run out from behind the woodpile and intercept the horse.

"What do you think you're doing?!" Frank shouts, running after you.

"Don't worry, I'll be right back," you say, leaping into the saddle.

"You're making a big mistake!" Frank shouts, as you start off in pursuit of the horseman with the woman's dresses.

The man is already at the edge of town and fast disappearing in the distance. You don't have any spurs, but you slap the horse on the side with your hand. "*Rápido*, quick!" you shout in its ear. The horse seems to understand and gallops faster.

As you leave the town behind you, the horseman is still up ahead. But you are gaining on him. His horse is just trotting along, while he sings a song in Spanish: "There were three señoritas / Sitting on one *silla* / Singing to each other / *Viva Pancho Villa.*"

You know that *silla* is a chair, but who is this Pancho Villa? you wonder.

→ → → → → → → → → → → →

Go on to the next page.

The horseman stops singing and gives you a surprised look as you come alongside. You reach over and grab the dresses draped over his arm. He grabs them back, and for a few moments there's a crazy tug-of-war. Then, the horseman almost loses his balance and lets go of the dresses. One of them flies up in the air and wraps itself around your head.

Suddenly you can't see anything. You try to pull the dress free. In the process, you lose your balance and pitch backward off the horse. You hit the ground lengthwise with a jarring thump, and for a moment you see stars.

You sit up groggily and free the dress from your head. Several horsemen have formed a circle around you, including the one you were after. They are all looking down at you and laughing.

One of them gets off his horse and comes over to you. "You very brave gringo, but very foolish. Now you come with us," he says.

The man points to your riderless horse. "I see you ride Pepé's horse. Ah, *muy triste*, very sad. But Pepé died bravely for the revolution."

You get on the horse and start off as you've been told. When you glance back, you see that the horseman behind you has taken his pistol from his holster and is keeping it trained on your back the whole time.

→ → → → → → → → → → → →

Go on to the next page.

Soon, you come to a high, barbed wire fence stretching into the distance on both sides. A large gap has been cut through it directly ahead.

"Aye, gringo, you are now in Chihuahua, Mexico," one of them says, when you are through the fence.

Well, you think, I wanted to see Mexico.

But you didn't mean this way.

You ride across the open desert for another hour, then start up into low, gravelly hills, with high mountains in the distance behind them. You spot white dots on the tops of the hills around you. You're surrounded by sentries on all sides.

You go over a rise and see a small valley ahead. In the center of it is what's left of a ranch. Several adobe buildings are there—minus their roofs. The remaining walls are fire-blackened.

A large corral to one side is intact and filled with horses. A number of ragged tents surround it.

You ride down to the encampment. There, you are ordered off your horse and your hands are tied in front of you. Then you are led around to the back of a building and shoved into one of the now-roofless rooms.

Two other captives, their hands also tied, are sitting on the floor with their backs against the wall. One, an overweight man in a disheveled suit, sits weeping quietly. He's either a businessman or a banker, you think. Next to him is an army officer in full uniform—a colonel as indicated by his insignia. He sits stoically, with a bemused look on his face. You sit next to him.

A guard stands by the door, rifle in hand.

"Hey, look," you call over in Spanish. "I have to be back in school in a few days."

The guard shrugs and shifts his rifle.

"Don't you understand? I'm going to miss school!" you plead.

"Ha, gringo," the guard finally replies, looking back out of the door for a few moments. "Soon I think you miss more than school. I see Cardenas, Villa's second-in-command, getting a little party ready for you three—a firing party."

The man in the suit whimpers. "For the love of God, I have a wife and children," he pleads in Spanish. "Please don't let them kill me."

"Say your prayers, old man," the guard says. "And on your feet. They are ready now."

The three of you are led outside and forced up against the wall of the house. A few yards away, several of the revolutionaries raise their rifles and point them in your direction.

Oh, great, you think, they're going to shoot me. What do I do?

→ → → → → → → → → → → →

Go on to the next page.

Suddenly a horseman reigns up between you and the riflemen. *"Suficiente!"* he shouts. "Enough blood for one day. Free those prisoners."

The members of the firing squad lower their rifles disappointedly.

The horseman—a tall, robust-looking man with a large, floppy mustache, dressed in a brown sweater, khaki trousers, and heavy riding boots—then gallops away to another part of the camp.

"Who is that?" you ask the guard, now coming over to you from a safe distance away.

"That is our general—General Francisco Villa," he says, as he unties your hands. "We know him as Pancho Villa. I see that he is feeling sentimental today."

"Vous avez de bonne chance, mon ami—you are lucky, my friend," another of the Villistas says, joining your group.

"Vous êtes francais?" you ask. "You are French?"

"Mais non, no, I am Belgian," he says. "And you speak French. *Formidable!* Terrific!"

"Indiana Jones, just down from Princeton, New Jersey," you introduce yourself, extending your hand.

"I am Remy Baudouin," he says in English, shaking your hand.

→ → → → → → → → → → → →

Go on to the next page.

"And I am José Gonzales from Ciudad Guerrero," the guard says.

"Is there any news of my country?" Remy asks you. "Is the war over?"

"The war is still going on," you say. "And the Germans still hold most of Belgium."

"Filthy swine!" Remy exclaims.

Suddenly a woman rider gallops into camp. All of you stop talking and watch as she leaps off her horse and runs over to Villa, now dismounted and standing some distance away. Immediately they get into a heated discussion. They are too far away for you to hear exactly what they are saying, but Villa is soon barking orders, and a wave of excitement spreads through the camp.

One of the Villistas runs up to José. "The Yankee General Pershing may cross the border at any time now and come after us," he says in Spanish. "Our general is not afraid of him, of course, but we are moving deeper into Chihuahua to be able to fight on a ground of our own choosing."

"I'll put you in one of the covered supply wagons," Remy tells you. "You'll be safe there—as long as you stay put. But if you try to escape, things could go badly for you."

Villa orders that everyone be fed before moving on. Remy brings you two freshly made tortillas and some chili sauce.

By the time the army of Villistas has packed up and is on the move, it is nearly sunset. The long line of horsemen, led by Villa himself, snakes out across the desert, followed by another line of supply wagons. You are so tired that you soon fall asleep in the back of one of them.

→ → → → → → → → → → → → →

Go on to the next page.

Sometime during the night, a particularly hard bump jars you awake. You lift the canvas at the back and look out into the darkness. You can hear the grinding of the wheels and the clip-clop of the horses' hooves, but you can't see anything except a few hazy stars above.

Perhaps now is a good time to make your escape. The wagon is not moving all that fast. You could easily jump to the ground and run off. On the other hand, you don't really know where you are. Maybe you should just stay put for the time being.

→ → → → → → → → → → → →

If you decide to jump out, turn to page 79.

← ← ← ← ← ← ← ← ← ← ← ←

If you decide to stay in the wagon, turn to page 9.

22

"**O**ver here!" you call to Frank, as you sprint to the woodpile, diving behind it. Frank's right with you. Seconds later, the horsemen gallop past, firing pistols and rifles in all directions. You can hear the bullets smacking into the other side of the woodpile. The horsemen are shouting, "*Viva Mexico! Viva Villa! Muerte a los Gringos!*"

You wait for a minute or so, then sneak a look through a narrow slit between the logs. You are just in time to see one of the horsemen toss something through the front window of the bank. Seconds later, there is an explosion inside. Several of the horsemen dismount and rush in.

Soldiers are now shooting back from the rooftops, and you see many of the horsemen topple from their saddles. You squeeze closer to the logs as some of those still riding toss burning torches through the windows of the hotel and the general store. Soon both buildings are on fire.

At the other end of the street, the men who went into the bank run out carrying thick saddlebags which you guess are stuffed with money.

← ← ← ← ← ← ← ← ← ← ← ← ←

Turn to page 10.

"Are those Americans?" you ask Remy.

"One of them is," Remy says. "He's a reporter from New York. The other man, the one with the metal claw, is named just that—Claw. He's an arms dealer specializing in dynamite."

"What happened to his hand?" you ask.

"I've been told it was blown off in an accident with his own merchandise," Remy says.

"The first man you mentioned, he's a reporter?"

"Oh, there are a lot of reporters around here, coming and going. We're big news up in the States. This one is a good friend of Villa. His name is John Reed."

"Maybe I could go over and talk with him," you say.

"You won't have to," Remy says. "He's coming over here."

"You look very familiar," Reed says to you as he arrives. "Something about . . ."

You introduce yourself. "I'm from Princeton, New Jersey," you explain. "My friends call me Indiana."

"Princeton! That's it. Your father must be a professor there."

"You know my father?"

"Not personally, I'm a Harvard man myself, but I've seen his picture in the papers. You look a lot like him. How did you come to be a Villista, might I ask?"

"I'm not," you say. "I was captured by Villa's

men outside Columbus and—"

"Captured, eh," Reed says. "I see we must have a talk with the general." He leads you over to where Villa is arguing with the man called Claw.

"The dynamite will cost you ten thousand American dollars," Claw says.

"Ten thousand? Impossible," Villa argues.

"I'm sorry," Claw says. "That is my price. After all, I need to make a profit on—"

"All right," Villa says. "I'll give you a thousand for a down payment. You'll get the rest in a week."

"In one week—no longer," Claw says as he walks off, snapping the blades of his artificial hand.

"Where are we going to get that kind of money?" Cardenas asks.

"In Ciudad Guerrero," Villa says.

"Ciudad Guerrero?" Cardenas asks.

"The *Federalistas* just shipped in a payroll. Two hundred thousand pesos in gold. Let's see, in dollars that's . . ."

"But general, Ciudad Guerrero is a fortress with thick walls and many soldiers."

Villa laughs. "The railroad, with the help of a little dynamite, can get through. We will give them one big surprise."

→ → → → → → → → → → → → →

Go on to the next page.

Villa notices you standing there. "And here is someone who has wandered into our midst. Are you with us or against us?"

"With you . . . I think. But I have to get back to school."

"School! There is nothing more important than school—except perhaps the revolution. Do you know what we are fighting for? I'll tell you— *Tierra y Libertad*—Land and Liberty."

Villa leans down and picks up a handful of earth. He holds it up so that it trickles through his fingers.

"*This* is what we are fighting for—for a man's right to own a piece of it, to raise his crops and feed his children. Isn't that right, *Chatito*," Villa says to John Reed, using the nickname "pug nose" that he's given him.

"Pancho *is* right," Reed says. "The so-called Mexican government—Carranza and his rich friends—is a puppet of the American president Woodrow Wilson. The plain, ordinary, hard-working people of Mexico have been reduced to pitiful, half-starved slaves in their own country. They own nothing and have no rights. If I weren't going off to cover the war against another tyranny in Europe, I would stay here and become a Villista myself."

→ → → → → → → → → → →

Go on to the next page.

"Well said!" Pancho Villa says, then turns to you. "Now go home—home to your fat, rich country, and your fat, rich life. Go home. I set you free."

You stand there stunned for a moment. You *do* have to get back to school. But if what they say is true, then perhaps you should help in the revolution.

→ → → → → → → → → → → → →

If you decide to go back to school,
turn to page 101.
If you decide to join the Villistas,
turn to page 45.

Deciding to stay with the Villistas, you and Remy watch as the long column of cavalry resumes its march around the the city. You help put José's body on the back of Remy's horse and mount up.

Just as you're starting off, you see a wagon surrounded by several dozen Villistas coming in your direction.

→ → → → → → → → → → → →
Go on to the next page.

When the mule-drawn wagon gets close, you recognize Pancho Villa propped up in the back. He waves for you to come alongside. You see that his lower leg is covered with blood-soaked bandages. He is obviously in great pain, but he does his best to talk. "We're headed to the mountains," he tells you and Remy. "I'll be safe there. I told the rest of *los hombres* to break up into small groups. We'll all meet at San Juan Bautista in a few weeks. But, Indy, you and Remy must stay with me."

As you are talking, shells whistle out of the sky and start to explode around you. Most of the Villistas scatter, but you and Remy stay with the wagon.

Fortunately you are soon out of range. You look back and see hundreds of Villistas fleeing through the opening in the wall.

→ → → → → → → → → → → → →

Turn to page 46.

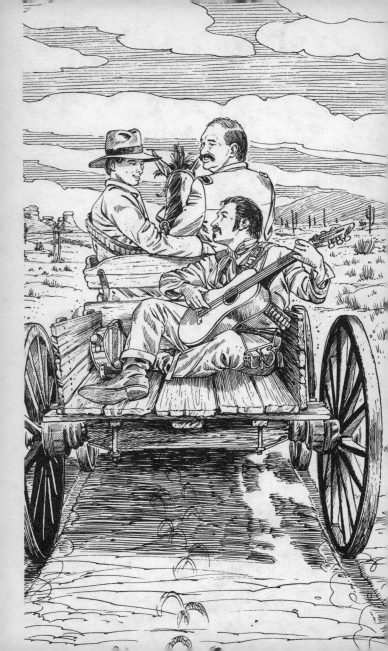

About noon, Remy goes off and comes back with a horse-drawn wagon. Both you and José jump on, and the wagon heads out of camp toward Claw's hacienda. José has brought his guitar.

You sit on the driver's bench next to Remy, while José strums the tune to "La Cucaracha," which seems to be the most popular song of the revolution.

"What I don't understand," you tell Remy in English, "is how you came to be riding with General Villa."

"I was a sailor," Remy says. One day, we tied up in Veracruz and I jumped ship. Then I met a woman named Lupé. I adored her, but the *Federalistas* killed her for criticizing the government. So, in her memory, I joined the revolution."

"For revenge?"

"No, not completely. You see I agree with Villa. I believe that this is a fight for justice, to recapture the land from the American imperialists and give it back to the Mexicans."

A couple of hours of bumping over the barely recognizable desert tracks brings you to Claw's hacienda, a forbidding-looking walled structure with a single entrance gate. From the outside it looks more like a fort.

$\rightarrow \quad \rightarrow \quad \rightarrow \quad \rightarrow \quad \rightarrow \quad \rightarrow \quad \rightarrow \quad \rightarrow \quad \rightarrow \quad \rightarrow \quad \rightarrow$

Go on to the next page.

Inside, it's not much prettier. A large, dark brown, two-story building is in the center of the enclosed space, surrounded by what might have once been gardens. Now they are just courtyards surfaced with reddish, horse-trampled earth. There are also scenes of feverish activity as dozens of peasants load machine guns and boxes of ammunition onto wagons and the backs of mules.

Claw appears at the door of the building, barking commands to the workmen—all the while snapping the two bladelike claws of his artificial hand open and closed.

"Hurry up!" he orders.

The workmen run into a side door of the building and reappear with large kegs labeled DYNAMITE in English on the sides. They load them into your wagon.

"All right, you're all loaded up," Claw says in Spanish. "When you deliver this to the general, remind him that I want the rest of the money in a week." Then he turns away and goes back into the building.

You start off in the cart, now loaded with a dozen large kegs of dynamite. José is driving, with Remy sitting beside him. You are squeezed into what little space is left in the back.

When the wagon finally reaches the outskirts of La Junta several hours later, you climb out, stiff from the cramped ride in the back.

"We'll leave the wagon here near the railroad tracks while we see if Cardenas is here," José says. "There's a cantina in the center of town."

"I hope they have something to eat," you say, as you head over toward it.

When you get to the cantina, the three of you sit at a table next to a large, open window. A blackboard over the bar announces that there is freshly made chili con carne on the menu. In fact, it's the only thing on the menu.

A while later, after you've finished eating, you see Cardenas and two other Villistas enter the cantina. Cardenas comes over to your table.

"I see you made it here without blowing yourselves up," he says in Spanish, and laughs. "I'll get a bit of refreshment, then we'll all go out and load the dynamite onto a flatcar waiting down the tracks."

Cardenas joins the other two Villistas at the bar.

A short time later, he is ready to go. Suddenly the swinging doors of the cantina fly open, and an American officer—a lieutenant—steps inside. Two ivory-handled .45s hang in holsters at his waist.

The officer walks to the bar, glancing at Cardenas and the others with a look of contempt, before half turning his back to them.

"Tequila," he says.

$\rightarrow$ $\rightarrow$ $\rightarrow$ $\rightarrow$ $\rightarrow$ $\rightarrow$ $\rightarrow$ $\rightarrow$ $\rightarrow$ $\rightarrow$ $\rightarrow$ $\rightarrow$ $\rightarrow$

Go on to the next page.

The barman, now sweating from fear, slides down a bottle. The officer pours himself a shot and tosses it down.

"God bless the U.S. of A., and death to her enemies—especially that dirty villain, Pancho Villa," he says.

There's a deathly silence. For a few moments, the room is like a picture suspended in time.

Then Cardenas and the two Villistas go for their guns. The officer's hands are a blur as he spins, draws both guns, and shoots from the hip.

Cardenas fires once, missing the officer but shattering the bottle of Tequila on the bar. The other two never get a chance to raise their guns.

Cardenas looks down, unbelieving, at the bullet hole square in the center of his chest. Then he crashes to the floor next to the bodies of the other two Villistas.

You can't believe what has just happened.

The officer twirls both guns on his trigger fingers, then places them neatly back in their holsters.

"Anyone else care to draw on George S. Patton?" he asks. "Guess not. Now help me get these bodies outside."

Patton directs you, José, and Remy to drape the bodies over the fenders of his large Dodge touring car parked just outside. Then he drives off.

→ → → → → → → → → → → →

Go on to the next page.

"Can you believe that?" you say.

"*Ese hombre es muy loco*," José says. "That man very crazy."

"Americans!" Remy says.

"What do we do now?" you ask.

"I guess we—" José starts to say, but is interrupted by the shrill whistle of a locomotive waiting just outside town.

You find a dozen Villistas sitting on it and a terrified engineer being held at gunpoint in the cab.

The dynamite is quickly transferred to a flatcar, which is then hooked up to the locomotive. Remy leaves the horse and wagon with the barman from the cantina, and the three of you climb on the flatcar. The train starts off, speeding along backward, pushing the flatcar in front of it.

Halfway to Ciudad Guerrero, the train meets Pancho Villa and several thousand of his men on horseback, all armed to the teeth. The train stops, and Villa climbs aboard.

"Where is Cardenas?" he asks.

"My General," José says. "I must sadly tell you that he died in a fierce engagement with the enemy."

None of you wants to tell Villa what really happened back in the cantina.

Villa takes off his hat and holds it to his chest. "Cardenas was a brave fighter," he says. "He will be well remembered when the final history of our glorious revolution is written."

"He will be," Remy says.

"But for now," Villa says, slapping his hat back on his head, "we have no time for tears. Many more will fall in the attack ahead of us."

You sure hope you're not one of them.

Villa gives a signal, and the train starts to move forward. The mass of Villistas gallop along beside it.

Villa pats one of the barrels of dynamite next to him. "Don't light the fuse until you are almost to the wall of the city," Villa says to Remy.

"Do the tracks go close enough?" Remy asks.

"There's a spur line that runs right up to the wall," José says. "I know. I grew up there."

"José, you switch the train over to the spur. I'll jump clear at the last moment," Remy says.

"Good!" Villa says. "Once we've blown a hole in the wall, the men, *los hombres*, will charge through. The city and the pesos will be ours."

Soon the city wall appears in the distance. The train slows down, and you, José, and Villa jump off. The Villistas have horses for the three of you.

"Be careful!" you call to Remy, as the train speeds up again, and you climb on your horse.

"Don't worry about me," Remy calls back. "I'll time it perfectly."

→ → → → → → → → → → → → →

Go on to the next page.

The locomotive rumbles along, pushing the flatcar with Remy and the dynamite in front of it. José gallops ahead at top speed, passing the train. He is almost to the switch that will send it hurtling toward the wall when he cries out and slumps across the saddle.

"Oh, no! José has been hit!" you cry out. You realize you're going to have to take care of the switch yourself.

You and your horse fly ahead like the wind. You pass the train and reach the switch with seconds to spare. Still mounted, you swing down from the saddle and grab the lever, pulling it forward.

The train lurches onto the spur line and speeds toward a wooden barrier a few yards from the base of the wall. Remy lights the short fuse on the dynamite and jumps clear. Ten seconds later, the train reaches the barrier, smashes through, and hurtles toward the wall.

Remy dashes back toward the switch. There is just time for you to help him swing up behind you, grab the reins of José's horse, and gallop to safety.

The shock wave from the explosion behind you nearly knocks you out of the saddle. Glancing back, you see that a wide section of the wall has been blasted open. Fragments of it, blown up into the sky, are still falling as the Villistas—led by Pancho Villa himself—charge through a thick cloud of dust into the city.

→ → → → → → → → → → → →

Go on to the next page.

You and Remy ease José down from his horse and put him gently on the ground. He groans.

"He's coming to," you say. "Easy, my friend."

José coughs and tries to speak. "Did someone throw the switch in time?" he asks in a low, weak voice.

"We did it," you say. "The dynamite blew a hole in the wall, and the Villistas are inside."

"Then I die happily. *Viva La Revolución!*" José says.

"Hold on. You'll be all right," you say.

But his head slumps back, lifeless.

"José, you can't die!" you cry out. But the sound of your voice is drowned out by the sudden roar of artillery nearby.

"Those sound like howitzers," Remy says. "They have to be those of either the *Federalistas* or the Americans. Either way it's not good."

A rider coming from the direction of the city gallops up. "The Yankees," he says in Spanish, "are counterattacking. There are too many of them. Villa has been wounded trying to assault the bank where the money is kept."

The rider gallops off as a large column of horsemen approaches from around the left side of the city. The lead horseman is carrying an American flag. Another carries a banner which reads: TROOP C—10TH CAVALRY.

The captain leading the column raises his hand. Looking back, he shouts, "Column halt! Ho!" They stop next to you.

→ → → → → → → → → → → → →

Go on to the next page.

Another officer looks down at José, not realizing he is dead. "Medic!" he calls down the line.

"It's too late," you say sadly.

The captain looks down at you quizzically. "I don't know which side you're on," he says, "but I think you'd better clear out of here fast. This sector is going to be raked by artillery fire."

"Thank you, sir," you say.

The death of José has made you reconsider what you're doing here. This whole revolution thing—is it worth it? you wonder. You have an impulse to jump on your horse and go off with the troopers. On the other hand, you *did* promise to help Villa. As the seconds tick away, you and Remy contemplate your options.

→ → → → → → → → → → → →

*If you decide to go with the troopers,
turn to page 103.*

← ← ← ← ← ← ← ← ← ← ← ←

*If you decide to stay with the Villistas,
turn to page 29.*

"I'd rather stay and help with the revolution," you say, deciding to join the Villistas.

A smile crosses Villa's face. *"Bueno—good!"* he says. "I have a special job for you—for you, José, and Remy. You'll take a wagon to Claw's hacienda and pick up the dynamite we'll need for the attack on Ciudad Guerrero. Then, you'll meet Cardenas, and the train, at La Junta."

"I must be going," John Reed says. "I have to be back in New York the day after tomorrow to catch a ship to Europe."

"Do you think the war there will be over soon?" Remy asks.

"Unfortunately, it looks like it's going to be a long, hard one. But perhaps it will be the war to end all wars."

"I hope we meet again someday," you say.

"Somehow, I'm sure we will," Reed says. "Until then, adios."

← ← ← ← ← ← ← ← ← ← ←

Turn to page 33.

The Americans apparently have surrounded the city and left open only a narrow corridor along which the Villistas are trying to escape. The shells exploding in their midst are taking a fearful toll.

You force yourself not to look back again. Your small group—the wagon and its driver, you and Remy, and two of the Villistas—heads across the trackless desert toward the mountains.

By nightfall, you reach a small village. It has been badly damaged. Bullet holes have riddled most of the walls, and some of the flimsy buildings have collapsed. Villa is carried inside one of the surviving huts.

There's a small graveyard near the town where you and Remy bury José.

"Adios and adieu, good friend," Remy says, standing by the grave. "Farewell."

You say your own silent prayer. Then you and Remy ride sadly back to the village.

As you approach it, one of the villagers comes out to meet you. "My name is Diego," he says in Spanish. "You must come to my house and be my guest."

When you get there, Diego's wife serves you and Remy a meal of tortillas and frijoles.

"Your general is in bad shape," Diego tells you. "A soft lead bullet has shattered the bone in his lower leg. We have no doctors here, of course, but one of the women has wrapped his wound with the peeled leaves of the nopal cactus. It is a good remedy, but she fears infection."

Suddenly you hear a commotion in the cobblestoned street outside. You and Remy run out. The two Villistas are walking away from the hut next door, each with a chicken slung over his shoulder. They are being followed by an old man. "Please! They're all I have," he pleads.

→ → → → → → → → → → → → →

Go on to the next page.

One of the Villistas looks back. "Hold your tongue. We can't fight on an empty stomach," he says.

You are about to go after the men and try to get the chickens back when Remy grabs your arm.

"No," he says. "They are heavily armed—and we must not begin fighting among ourselves. We have the general to look after."

"But Remy . . ."

Remy sighs. *"Mais oui, c'est dommage,"* he says. "It's a pity."

Remy goes over to comfort the old man. He takes some silver coins out of his pocket and gives them to him. "I'm sorry about your chickens," Remy says.

"Muchas gracias, señor. I thank you for the money sir, but there is no need to apologize. It is always the same. In the revolution, it is the people who suffer."

"But it's the people we're fighting for," you say.

→ → → → → → → → → → → →

Go on to the next page.

"Listen," the old man says. "Many years ago, I rode with Juárez against the emperor Maximilian. During that time, I lost many chickens, but I thought it was worth it to be free. When Díaz became president, I supported him, but his men stole my chickens. So I supported Madero, who they killed. Then they put in Huerta whose people came and stole my chickens. When Carranza took over after him, they stole my chickens. Now Pancho Villa has come to liberate me, and the first thing his men do is take my chickens."

You and Remy go back in the house. You both sit there silently for a while, thinking.

The old man is probably right, you realize. Revolutions come and go, presidents come and go. The only thing that changes is the name of the man who steals from the people.

Early the next morning, you are all ready to start off again. "Farewell," Diego says, as he gives you and Remy a stack of fresh tortillas for the trip, wrapped in a sheet of newspaper.

You thank all the villagers and start out behind the wagon carrying Villa, heading out toward the mountains, now much closer.

Later, around noon, when you stop to rest, Remy unwraps the tortillas and spreads out the sheet of newspaper. It's a front page, and only a few months old. "I wonder where Diego got this. I doubt if he can read."

The main headline in Spanish reads:

TWO YEARS OF CONFLICT
EUROPE STILL LOCKED IN DEADLY STRUGGLE.

Underneath is a picture showing soldiers with gas masks and bayonets charging across a shell-torn, almost lunar landscape. Shells are seen exploding in the distance. The caption reads *Waves of German troops advance through no-man's-land.*

"As soon as we get the general to safety, I'm going home," Remy says. "If I'm going to die, I want to die defending my own country."

"You're right," you say. "And I'm going with you."

Remy laughs. *"Tu es fou, mon ami,"* he says.

"I am not crazy," you say. "Your people must be liberated. It's as important to my country as it is to yours."

After eating, you start off again. Late in the afternoon, you start up into the mountains. The sky is now leaden gray, and the weather has turned cold and bitter. Snow starts to fall.

Suddenly the wagon carrying Villa begins to slip sideways toward the edge of the steep, now-slippery trail.

"Quick! Help with the general!" one of the Villistas calls out.

→ → → → → → → → → → → → →

Go on to the next page.

You and Remy dismount and run up to the wagon. Remy jumps on board and heaves Villa, now half-conscious and delirious, over the side. As he does, you grab the general and ease him to the ground.

Remy jumps off just as the wagon slips off the edge of the trail and goes crashing down a steep slope.

You and Remy fashion a litter of saplings from along the side of the road and carry Villa further up the trail. Here, the entrance to a large cave is completely hidden by thick brush.

Inside, it's dry and warmer. Villa falls into a deep sleep. You, Remy, and the Villistas also manage to rest.

Early the next morning, an American patrol passes so close to the cave that you can hear them singing, "It's a Long Way to Tipperary," a song about the war in Europe. But the troopers, riding their horses through the freshly fallen snow, fail to notice any of you or the cave itself.

For the next few days you hide there, rationing your food and obtaining water from melted snow. Gradually the sky clears, and miraculously enough, Villa starts to recover. Soon he is hobbling about with a cane.

When you and Remy realize that Villa is out of danger, you both quietly slip away one moonlit night while the rest are sleeping. You ride all the way to the coast, carefully avoiding the guer-rillas and the Americans hunting for them.

You and Remy take a boat from Veracruz.

"I hope you Americans will help liberate my country," Remy says.

→ → → → → → → → → → → →

Go on to the next page.

"I know that we will," you say.

You both sit on deck for a long while, silently gazing out over the ocean. You know that people like you and Remy will always stand together in defense of freedom.

In the meantime, the ship steams on—headed back toward home.

The End

You decide to go between the buildings.

"This way, quick!" you shout to Frank, as you head for the narrow walkway between the stable and the forge. You squeeze inside, with Frank close behind. As you do, the horsemen thunder past, firing their guns in all directions.

Fortunately, it's still dark in the walkway, and none of the horsemen notices you as they gallop by. There is just enough space for you and Frank to squeeze through to the back of the buildings.

The din carries over the rooftops from the main street, but the back lane is still peaceful. Several dirt roads lead away from where you are standing. They are lined with a scattering of ramshackle houses. Here and there, points of light from oil lamps inside pierce the early morning gloom.

You and Frank walk rapidly along one of the back streets leading north and out of town. After a while, the sound of gunfire fades behind you, and the street feeds into what passes for the main road.

You look back and see that the central part of the town is on fire. A cloud of thick smoke rises over it.

→ → → → → → → → → → → → →

Go on to the next page.

The sky is much brighter now. You see a large cavalry detachment galloping toward you from the north. You get off on the side of the road as they go past. It takes a few minutes for the column of several hundred troopers to pass. When the dust has settled, you start off again.

Then you see something else coming from the north. It's a large touring car, painted army brown, barreling down the road. It slows and stops in front of you.

"Are you from Columbus?" a soldier asks, leaning out the window.

"We just came from there. We saw part of the attack on the town," you say. "The horsemen were shouting, 'Viva Villa,' whatever that means."

"It means that Pancho Villa has finally done it," the soldier says. "He's attacked the United States."

"We should get back and tell General Pershing about this right away," the soldier next to him—a corporal—says.

"You don't want to recon further ahead?" the first soldier asks.

"No time," the corporal says. He turns to you and Frank. "Can you come with us and tell the general what you saw?"

"Sure," you say. Frank also nods.

"Jump in, then."

You and Frank climb into the wide, leather-covered seats in the back. The car makes a U-turn and speeds north.

"Wait until General Pershing hears about this," the corporal says. "He's going to be as mad as a wet hen. Villa's in big trouble. By the way, my name is Corporal Poole, and this is Private Morris driving."

You and Frank introduce yourselves.

"I don't know anything about this Pancho Villa. Or General Pershing, for that matter," Frank says.

"Well, let me tell you about Pershing," Poole says. "Thirty years ago, as a junior cavalry officer, he hunted down renegade Apache Indians in this same territory. Later he was in the charge up San Juan Hill in Cuba during our war with Spain. Still later, he subdued the fierce Moro tribes on the island of Mindanao in the Philippines. As you can see, he's not someone you want to mess around with."

"It sure seems that way!" you say.

"President Theodore Roosevelt made him a general, jumping over the heads of eight hundred officers more senior, most of whom are still hopping mad about it."

"And I'm going to meet him?" you say.

"You bet," Poole says.

"What about this guy Villa?" Frank asks. "Who is Pancho Villa?"

$\rightarrow$ $\rightarrow$ $\rightarrow$ $\rightarrow$ $\rightarrow$ $\rightarrow$ $\rightarrow$ $\rightarrow$ $\rightarrow$ $\rightarrow$ $\rightarrow$ $\rightarrow$

Go on to the next page.

"Villa killed his first government official at sixteen, then became a bandit for the next twenty years," Poole says. "Later, when things got too hot for him, he hid out in El Paso in the States. He returned to Mexico when he saw his chance to become a big revolutionary leader."

"Why would people follow a guy like that?" you ask.

"When he was an outlaw, he built up this image of himself as robbing from the rich and giving to the poor—like Robin Hood."

"Did he?" Frank asks.

"He could have," Poole says. "But now it looks like he's shown his true colors."

After driving for an hour, you get to Pershing's headquarters. In front, as you turn off the road, are several very long, one-story buildings—permanent barracks built of brick and adobe. Off to the side is a small city of army tents next to a large drill field.

At the far end of the field, there's a long line of mule-drawn pack wagons, each covered with a semicircular canvas cover. They remind you of the Conestoga wagons the pioneers used to cross the plains. Next to them is a smaller row of big trucks, looking not much different from the wagons but with motors in front instead of mules.

Way over on the far side are eight boxy-looking double-winged planes. A strip of smoothed land stretches away from them into the surrounding desert.

Corporal Poole takes you and Frank to the headquarters building and into Pershing's office. General Pershing and a lieutenant are standing in front of a wall-mounted map of Mexico, Texas, and the Southwest.

The corporal salutes snappily. "Corporal Poole reporting, sir. Encountered these two civilians on the road outside Columbus. They witnessed an attack by Villa's forces on the town."

You and Frank tell what you saw to the lieutenant and the general.

→ → → → → → → → → → → →

Go on to the next page.

Pershing walks over to his desk and slams down his fist. "Villa! That low-down miserable skunk. I'll nail his hide to the wall."

"Let's go after him at once," the lieutenant says.

"If only we could," Pershing says. "I'm still waiting for permission from Washington to cross the border."

"But sir, this is an actual invasion of the United States."

"I know, Lieutenant Patton, but with the war spreading in Europe, President Wilson is worried about getting into one with Mexico."

"We can't just sit here and do nothing," Patton says.

"I expect word from Washington at any moment. The president is pressuring the Mexican government for permission to go into its territory. Until then—" He shrugs.

"I can scout along the border," Patton suggests. "Villa may strike again."

"Good idea," Pershing says. "Also, we're running low on food here at the camp. There's a large ranch to the west that spans the border. It belongs to that newspaper publisher Hearst. Take a mounted patrol out there. See what supplies they can give us, and pick up whatever information you can about Villa's movements."

→   →   →   →   →   →   →   →   →   →   →

Go on to the next page.

"If I may suggest another idea, General," Patton says. "I'd like to take several automobiles."

"Do you think that's wise? Motorized vehicles have never been tried in this kind of operation," Pershing says.

"That's just why I'd like to try it. It's something I've been thinking about. Sort of a 'mechanized warfare.'"

"Okay," Pershing says. "We may need some original ideas when we're called on to help out in Europe."

"Do you really think we will be?" you ask.

"I have no doubt of it," Pershing says.

"We'll be ready," Patton says.

"Oh, and when you go on this patrol, take someone along who can speak Spanish, a civilian if necessary," Pershing says.

"I can speak Spanish, sir," you say. "I speak several languages, actually. May I go along?"

"Hey, wait a minute, Indy," Frank says. "We're supposed to be getting back to school."

"Is that true?" Pershing asks.

"Well, sort of," you say.

"Then I suggest that you think carefully about this. I can't guarantee how long this operation will last."

"I don't know about you," Frank says, "but I'm going back. I've had enough of those Mexican bandits, or whatever they are."

You feel you should go back with Frank. On the other hand, things are beginning to get exciting down here. You hate to pass up the opportunity to go on the mission with Patton.

→ → → → → → → → → → → →

If you decide to go on the mission with Patton, turn to page 88.
If you decide to go back with Frank, turn to page 102.

You tell Juan that you've decided to take the train to Mexico City. About noon, an elegant horse-drawn coach pulls up in front of Lorenzo's house. In addition to you and Juan, one of Lorenzo's daughters, Rosita, a girl about the same age as you, is making the trip. She is going to Mexico City to study piano at the conservatory of music. Lorenzo and his wife come along to see you all off.

The train station is a small shack with a water tower next to it, a mile out of town. The three of you get out of the coach and wait by the tracks. You see the plume of smoke from the train when it's still a long way off. Then, some minutes later, you see it way down the tracks. Finally it comes to a stop in the station with a hiss of steam and a squeal of brakes.

You thank Lorenzo and his wife for their hospitality and climb aboard. You sit next to Juan, with Rosita opposite you across the aisle. The train, wasting no time, starts off.

"How do you like our country?" Rosita asks you in Spanish.

→ → → → → → → → → → → →

Turn to page 89.

"As far as cars are concerned, do you think it's a good idea to charge the enemy in them?" you ask.

"Not right now," Patton says. "But with steel plate wrapped around them and Gatling guns mounted on top, they might be powerful weapons. Do you know about the *Monitor* in the Civil War?"

"That was an ironclad ship, wasn't it?"

"Right. But what if we could have some kind of armored ships on land?"

"They'd be too heavy. The wheels would just sink into the ground," you say.

"Railroad locomotives are heavy, but they don't sink."

"That's because they run on tracks," you say.

"What if our land-ship carried its own tracks? They could run in a continuous circle all the way around the tires," Patton says.

"I guess they could—" you start to say when suddenly you see something up ahead. "Look! A column of smoke," you shout. "It looks like the one I saw over Columbus after Villa's men set it on fire."

"There's no town there, at least not one that's marked on the map," Patton says. "But there *is* the Hearst hacienda."

You drive another twenty minutes. When you're closer to the source of the smoke, Patton stops the car on the side of the road.

"If Villa is attacking, I don't want to run into an ambush," Patton says. "The land rises off to the left over there. Let's go up and take a look."

Patton takes a pair of binoculars from the glove compartment, and you both start up the gentle slope. He ducks down as you reach the ridge at the top, training his binoculars on the country-side ahead.

From the ridge, the land extends out in a wide sweep of desert all the way to the distant mountains. In the near distance is a large hacienda. It is surrounded by a high wall, and one of its buildings is on fire. Horsemen, firing rifles from the saddle, are circling it like hostile Indians surrounding a wagon train.

"Is there anything we can do?" you ask.

"Hmmmm. Must be several hundred men down there—probably Villa's. We're outnumbered about a hundred to one. But I wouldn't let that bother me if I had enough ammunition."

You watch as an explosion blows open the front gate and the horsemen charge into the hacienda. A short time later, a number of them come back out on foot, carrying large sacks full of loot—probably silverware, jewelry, and fancy clothes. Several are struggling to pull out a grand piano. Seeing that the task is hopeless, they start to smash the instrument to pieces with their rifle butts. The twang of the snapping strings sends a crazy musical sound across the desert.

"Shouldn't we drive back to headquarters and get the cavalry?" you ask.

"The varmints would be long gone by the time it got here," Patton says. "But we'll get them sooner or later. We'll keep an eye on them and see which way they go."

→ → → → → → → → → → → →

Go on to the next page.

An hour later all the gunmen have disappeared into the distance to the southwest. Nothing is left of the hacienda but smouldering ruins. There is no sign of life, at least from a distance.

"We'll drive over there and see if anyone is still alive," Patton says, as you go back down the slope to where the rest of the men are sitting on the ground in the shade of the cars. As Patton arrives, they jump to attention.

Suddenly you hear a buzzing sound high up in the sky. You use your hand to shade your eyes from the sun as you look up. Patton does the same.

"Looks like one of our JN–4s," Patton says. "The pilots have nicknamed them 'flying Jennies.'"

The plane gets closer. Finally it dives and swoops by, a hundred feet or so over your heads. Patton waves his arms, and the pilot, leaning out of his open cockpit, waves back.

The plane circles once around and comes in for a landing on a stretch of road up ahead, then taxis near the cars. The pilot climbs down and strides over.

"Ah, Captain Smith! What brings you out our way?" Patton asks.

→ → → → → → → → → → → → →

Go on to the next page.

"The general thought I might fly here and see if your vehicles had made it to the hacienda," Captain Smith replies. "I suspect he wants to see if I can make it this far myself. He has little confidence in my Jenny here."

"There's not much left of the hacienda. The men that attacked it were most likely Villa's," Patton says.

"I must say that the view of it from the air looks pretty desolate," says Captain Smith. "I followed the trail of smoke all the way out. Spotted a column of horsemen off to the southwest. They seemed to be breaking up into smaller groups."

"In that event, no use going after them now," Patton says.

"Either of you care for a ride back? I have an empty seat in the cockpit."

"I have to go over to what's left of the hacienda and see if anyone is still alive. But my interpreter here might want to give it a try," Patton says, turning to you.

"How about it?" Smith says. "It's safe enough. My friends joke that my plane has all the gliding characteristics of a brick. But I've crash-landed three times and suffered hardly a scratch."

"I'll give it a try," you say.

"Climb in behind me then, and fasten your safety belt."

You say good-bye to Lieutenant Patton and climb aboard the Jenny.

The plane bounces down the road a short distance. Then, leaving the ground, it glides smoothly up into the air. The wind blowing in your face feels good.

You look down and back and watch as the cars and soldiers on the ground quickly become small dots far below. Smith gives a thumbs-up from the open cockpit in front.

The view from above seems to magnify the desolation of the desert. It's a vast wasteland of dried-out riverbeds and sand dunes. In the distance, the ruler-straight line of the railroad cuts across the landscape from north to south.

Soon you see the sprawling army base up ahead. The plane swoops down and levels out a few feet above the ground, going in for a landing.

You feel the bump as the wheels touch down. The plane bounces along, still moving rapidly.

→ → → → → → → → → → → →

Go on to the next page.

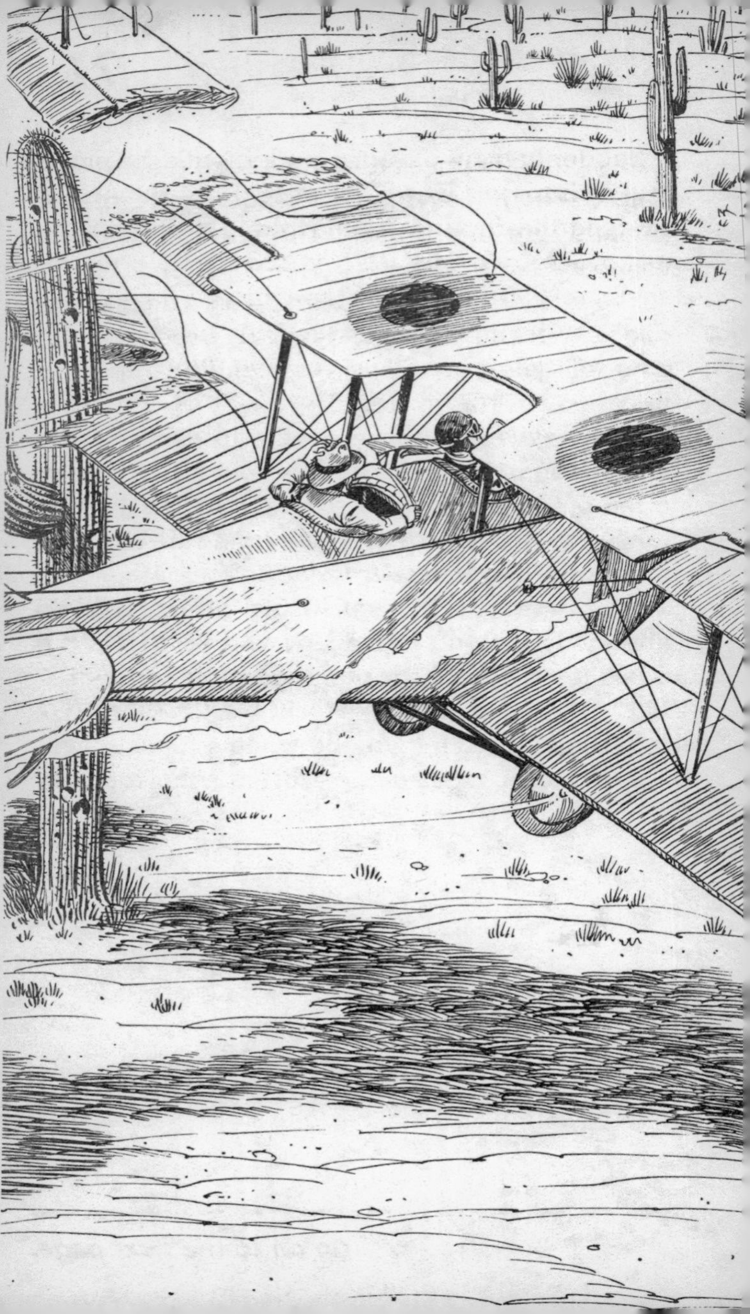

Suddenly there's a bang underneath the plane and a sharp jolt. The right wing drops down and scrapes the ground as the plane spins off the narrow runway. A tall yucca cactus neatly shears off half of one of the wings.

General Pershing and several other officers from headquarters come running over.

"What happened *this* time, Smith?" he says, looking disgusted, as you and Smith climb down from what's left of the plane.

"A little trouble with the landing gear, I suspect," Smith says, bending down to look under the wreckage. "I think we hit a rut."

Pershing starts to walk away angrily but then stops and turns back. "Glad you both made it down all right," he says. He gestures for you to follow as he continues back to the headquarters building.

→ → → → → → → → → → → →

Go on to the next page.

"I've given your situation some thought," Pershing says to you back in the office. "With your talent for languages and your natural spunk, you'd be perfect for military intelligence."

"A spy?" you say.

"Maybe," Pershing says. "Or you might be attached to headquarters for analyzing intelligence information, breaking codes, that sort of thing. But for now, I think it best that you get back and finish your education while you can. We'll all be needed soon to stop the spreading tyranny in Europe. I'm putting you on the afternoon train going north."

"Tell Lieutenant Patton good-bye for me," you say. "I wish I could tell him in person, but I didn't realize I'd be leaving like this."

"I will," Pershing says.

An hour later, you are on a train heading home to New Jersey. You think about what General Pershing said about the war in Europe. You wonder if your country really will become part of it. Right now, the best thing for you to do would be to finish school, as General Pershing said.

But to become a spy? That *would* be exciting, you think, as the train rolls north across the country.

The End

You decide to jump out of the wagon. You carefully lift the canvas flap and let your legs dangle over the back rail of the wagon for a few moments. Then you push free.

You hit the ground running and dash off the road, brushing past a cactus in the darkness. Its needles grab at your clothes. You stop and crouch down, your heart pounding, and let the rest of the wagons rumble past you in the darkness. The sounds of the wagons are followed by the clip-clop of horses' hooves as they all fade off into the distance.

You sit down on the ground, shivering a bit. Soon the silence is complete. You lie back with your hands behind your head, remembering another great silence in the Egyptian desert. Your friends were with you then. But now you are completely alone.

The ground is warmer than the air. You turn over and hug it for warmth, dozing off after a while.

→ → → → → → → → → → → → →

Go on to the next page.

In the morning, when the fiery red sun shoots up over the horizon, you find that you are no longer completely alone. You are surrounded by several curled-up rattlesnakes.

Ugh, snakes! If there's anything you hate, it's snakes! You jump up and carefully thread your way around them back to the road.

From where the sun is rising in the east, you know that the road runs north and south. You decide to head north toward the border.

You walk for hours through the sandy wastes, the relentless sun beating down on you. Shimmering mirages cloud your vision. Fortunately, you still have your hat, which you've kept through it all. At least your head and face are protected.

You are hungry, but most of all, you are thirsty. Your throat is so dry that you can hardly swallow—and you feel your body being quickly dehydrated. Your legs are like lead. High in the air, a pair of buzzards circles, waiting for you to drop.

You are about to give up hope when you see a small village in the distance. You call on your last reserve of energy and make it to the edge of town. You slump down in the shade of the first building.

→ → → → → → → → → → → →

Go on to the next page.

Several of the villagers see you and run over. In a few minutes a small crowd has gathered around. A woman brings you a cup of water, while another fans you with a large hat.

"Do not drink it down all at once," the woman says in Spanish. "First, just wet your mouth, then sip it slowly."

"*Gracias*," you say, and do as she says. You look around at the buildings. There are a few gouges in the walls that could be bullet holes, but otherwise the town seems in pretty good shape. You wonder how they've managed that, with all the fighting going on.

Two of the townspeople help you get up and then guide you to the local cantina.

"My name is Juan, Juan Moracho," one of them says in Spanish, as you sit down. "Are you an American?"

"*Si . . . Americano*," you say.

"Ha! I thought so," Juan says, switching to English. "Your country not too popular south of the border. They are afraid that you will invade and take another big piece of land away from us like you did with Texas, California, New Mexico, and Arizona."

"I don't know about that," you say. "I'm from New Jersey. I just want to get back home."

The waiter brings you a glass of something. Several people look at you expectantly as you drink it down. Whatever it is, it burns like fire.

→ → → → → → → → → → →

Go on to the next page.

"Is that tequila?" you ask.

"No, my friend, that is sotol, the fruit of the cactus," Juan says. "It is good, no?"

"How far am I from the border?" you ask, shaking your head.

"Not too far. About a hundred miles," Juan says. "But if you are thinking of trying to ride there, forget it. If the *Federalistas* catch you, they will kill you. If the Villistas catch you, they will kill you too."

"Maybe I'll find some Americans?"

"I do not think so, amigo."

"Then I'm stuck here," you say. "Am I safe? You said everyone here was mad at the United States."

Juan laughs. "They will not hold it against you personally. Every person is judged on his own merits. Do not worry, tomorrow we can put you on the train for Mexico City."

"I don't want to go to Mexico City, I want—"

"As you wish," Juan says. "But consider it carefully. It may be the safest way for you. Villa is raiding in the north and Zapata is raiding in the south. In between, it is fairly safe. By coincidence, I am also going to Mexico City tomorrow. I have business there."

"But what do I do when I get to Mexico City?" you ask. "I'll be even further away from home than I am now."

"From there you can get a stagecoach to Veracruz, and from there a boat to the States. You see it will be very easy. Come, you can stay with my friend Lorenzo until then."

You follow Juan out of the cantina and through a number of the twisting, cobblestoned streets. Many of the buildings have finely cut stonework, and in places over the street they have overhangs. They remind you of the old section of Cairo in Egypt.

Finally you go through a door in a faceless red wall fronting the street and into a flower-filled courtyard with a fountain in the center.

A tile roof held up by a long row of elegant arches covers a wide porch that runs all the way around the garden.

"Lorenzo, someone is here to see you," Juan calls out.

A short, dark-haired man with a neatly trimmed mustache and goatee appears from the house behind the garden. "Ah, Juan and the American! You are most welcome in my home," he says in slightly accented English.

Word must get around fast in this town, you realize.

Standing behind Lorenzo is an attractive woman with long, jet-black hair. She is wearing a colorful, finely woven blouse and a long white skirt.

→ → → → → → → → → → → → →

Go on to the next page.

"Let me introduce my wife, Margarita," Lorenzo says.

"How do you do," Margarita says. "We lived a few years in your country. Such a beautiful place, and such wise people."

"Thank you," you say, and then introduce yourself.

"I've come to see if you have any ideas on how to get our new friend here back home," Juan says. "I've suggested that Indy first take the train to Mexico City."

"That would be one way," Lorenzo says. "A little roundabout."

"Perhaps you have another idea," Juan says.

"I have a friend, Manuel Gamio, an archaeologist. I'm sort of his unofficial patron. I am about to send some supplies to him up in the mountains. There is a pyramid there that he is excavating. There is also an American archaeologist, a Mr. Morley, working with him. They go back and forth between Mexico and the United States with the official sanction of the government."

"How soon could our friend get home from there?"

"That I do not know," Lorenzo says. "In any event, Indy doesn't have to decide today. You are welcome to stay here as long as necessary."

"You see, Indiana, I leave you in good hands," Juan says, as he says good-bye to his friends.

"We were just about to have our main meal of

the day," Lorenzo says. "I would be honored if you would be our guest."

Besides Lorenzo and his wife, there are two sets of grandparents and half a dozen children of all ages at the very large dinner table. You notice that the meal—fish, steak, and vegetables as well as the traditional beans, corn, and chili— is put on the table by several servants. They seem happy enough, really part of the family.

That night you sleep in a large guest room on the second floor.

Juan comes by after breakfast in the morning to see what you've decided to do.

← ← ← ← ← ← ← ← ← ← ← ←
*If you decide to take the train to Mexico City,
turn to page 66.*

→ → → → → → → → → → → →
*If you decide to go to the archaeological site,
turn to page 97.*

"**I**'m going with you on the mission," you say to Patton.

"Welcome aboard," the lieutenant says, giving you a quick salute.

You say good-bye to Frank, and an hour later, three Dodge touring cars pull up in front of headquarters. There are two corporals, a sergeant, and six privates distributed among the cars. Patton takes over the controls of the lead car, and you jump in beside him.

Patton wastes no time. He throws the car into gear and speeds out of camp, with the other two cars following close behind.

You drive on a dirt road that goes along the border, keeping a lookout for any human activity.

"I'm afraid that General Pershing has little faith in the future of mechanized warfare," Patton says. "He still prefers the horse cavalry. He cares even less about the airplanes."

"I saw a number of them at the base," you say.

"I'll have to admit that they don't look too promising—just large motorized box kites made of cloth stretched on flimsy wooden frames. But I think there will be big improvements. Someday airplanes may play a large role in warfare."

← ← ← ← ← ← ← ← ← ← ←
Turn to page 68.

"To be truthful," you say, "I haven't seen much of it except for the desert."

"Then you have a lot to see yet," Rosita says. "Mexico is the most beautiful country in the world. It has tropical coasts with wide beaches and high, snow-covered mountains. Did you know that? You will be able to see some of these mountains from Mexico City. We also have many splendid cities, with palaces and great cathedrals."

"I hope none of them will be destroyed in the fighting that's going on," you say.

"All this chaos will pass," Juan says. "We are a new nation in the throes of being born. There will soon be an end to this terrible revolution. Villa and Zapata, calling themselves liberators, will not succeed in destroying those of us who have educated ourselves and worked for stability."

→ → → → → → → → → → → →

Go on to the next page.

"I was captured by Villa and his men," you say. "But I escaped."

"Thank goodness you escaped!" Rosita exclaims.

"Who is this Zapata you mentioned?" you ask.

"He is an *indio*, an Indian, who has raised an army of other *indios* and mestizos, those of mixed blood, in the southern state of Morelos. They have seized much land and burned many haciendas. Two years ago, Villa and Zapata joined forces and occupied Mexico City itself. But their partnership, and the occupation of the city, did not last very long. It is one thing to be clever guerrillas, and another when it comes to governing a country."

The train crosses the desert for hours, then starts up into a range of mountains. Often the grade is so steep that the train just creeps along, struggling every inch of the way. Sometimes you look out the window and see nothing but space where the tracks are cut into the mountainside— a vertical drop of hundreds of feet only inches away.

When night comes, you look out into total blackness. You do your best to try to sleep.

The next morning, the train descends into a broad valley.

"We are now in the Valley of Mexico," Rosita says. "The city is not far."

In the distance, the surface of a lake shimmers in the morning sun.

"That is Lake Texcoco," Rosita says. "It was once much larger. The Aztecs built their capital, Tenochtitlán, on an island in the center of it. Mexico City stands in the same location, but it is now part of the mainland."

Suddenly the train whistle blows several times, and the train screeches to a stop. You look out the window and see that it is surrounded by hundreds of horsemen, all wearing the same outfits of white trousers, white shirts, and broad-rimmed, high-crowned hats.

"Those are the *campesinos*, the peasant army of Zapata," Juan says.

"They will kill us all!" Rosita says, starting to sob into her handkerchief.

"I don't think they will," Juan says. "But still, we must be brave."

Everyone is ordered out of the train and made to stand along the tracks. The passengers all have looks of fear on their faces, and many are crying. The *campesinos*, on the other hand, are smiling and joking to each other as they ride up and down the tracks brandishing their guns.

Then the line of horsemen parts, and a slender, dark-skinned rider with a drooping mustache gallops up to the train on a large, white horse.

"That's Zapata himself," Juan whispers to you. "I wonder why he's so close to the city."

All the Zapatistas now look serious. There is complete silence except for the low sobs of some of the passengers.

Zapata reins his horse to a stop and looks up and down the line of people assembled by the train. His eyes are dark and penetrating.

→ → → → → → → → → → → →

Go on to the next page.

"I will tell you this," Zapata says in a low but distinct voice. "The leaders in Mexico City are traitors to the revolution. We must have a *new* revolution. We must take back the land that was stolen from us. Carranza promised us freedom, but he has betrayed us to the large landowners. The nation must be ruled by the true Mexicans, the Indians and the mestizos, not the Americans, and not the corrupt descendants of the conquistadores. These people sleep in soft beds and know nothing of the suffering of the peasants. Now back on your train and tell them in Mexico City what I, Emiliano Zapata, have said."

Zapata turns his horse and gallops off, followed by the rest of the *campesinos*.

"That was really something!" you say, as you get back on the train.

"Don't believe a word of it," Juan says. "They say that Zapata is incorruptible and wants nothing for himself. That's what they all say until they are in total control."

"Praise to God! We're all safe," Rosita says. "I was so scared."

An hour later, the train pulls into a large station in the city.

When you get outside, Rosita points out the three white peaks of Ixtáccihuatl Mountain off in the distance.

"Maybe you thought I was joking when I told

you of snow-covered mountains in my country. Well, there they are," she says.

"They *are* beautiful," you say.

"Thank you," Rosita says. "Now I must be off to school."

Later, Juan arranges for a stagecoach to take you to Veracruz. But first he takes you on a tour of the city, one full of magnificent Spanish-colonial architecture. You also wonder what the Aztec capital must have been like.

A few days later, you take a boat from Veracruz, heading back to New Jersey. Although this adventure is over, you feel certain you'll have many others in the days and years ahead.

The End

You tell Juan that you've decided to visit the archaeological site.

You stay with Lorenzo for the next couple of days. Then, early one morning, he takes you out to the edge of town where a packtrain of mules is being loaded. There are several mule drivers on horseback, and an extra horse is waiting for you.

"I have a feeling that you and my friend Manuel will get along quite well," Lorenzo says, as he says good-bye. "Visit us again someday, if you can."

You thank him and start off with the packtrain.

Once again you head out across the desert. You are tempted to break away and gallop toward the north and the border. It might be worth the chance. But then you realize that it would be an insult to Lorenzo after all his kindness.

Soon, however, you find yourself going into the mountains. After many hours of traveling, you come to a high, brush-covered plateau.

In the center is a large, earth-covered mound, roughly the shape of a pyramid. One side of it has been excavated. A stone stairway, running from top to bottom, has been exposed.

Two men, one very short and American-looking with thick glasses and a straw hat, and the other a Mexican, are working with shovels at the base.

→ → → → → → → → → → → → →

Go on to the next page.

They stop and come over as the mules arrive at their camp. One of the mule drivers, apparently on instructions from Lorenzo, explains to them why you are along.

"I am Manuel Gamio," the Mexican says. "And this is my American associate, Sylvanus Morley."

You introduce yourself.

"Unfortunately neither of us will be going back to the States for a few weeks," Manuel says. "Are you interested in archaeology?"

"Very," you say. "I've visited the pyramids and other archaeological sites in Egypt. Have you ever heard of Howard Carter?"

"Oh, yes," Manuel says. "I read about him in an archaeological journal while I was studying at Columbia University in your country. He's searching in the Valley of the Kings for the tomb of Tutankhamen, I believe."

"That's right. I was with him when he discovered the first clue to its whereabouts, a small fragment of pottery with Tutankhamen's royal seal."

"Extraordinary!" Sylvanus exclaims. "Then you'll fit right in here. We've just discovered a whole new Mexican civilization that seems to predate all the known ones, including, of course, the Aztecs."

"I know something about the Aztecs," you say. "They were destroyed by the Spanish not many years after Columbus discovered America."

"That's right," Manuel says. "Hernán Cortés and a gang of four hundred Spaniards landed near what is now Veracruz in 1519. They had fourteen horses and a number of canon. With these, they crossed two mountain passes ten thousand feet high to get to the Aztec capital of Tenochtitlán in the Valley of Mexico."

"And this small number of men defeated the entire Aztec nation?" you ask.

"In fact," Manuel says, "in their first skirmish they were almost all wiped out. They retreated and returned a year later with ten thousand native allies happy to rebel against the Aztecs. Little did they know that the Spanish would prove to be as brutal as their former masters. After a seventy-five-day siege, the capital—a Venice-like city in the center of a large lake—fell to the Spaniards and their allies. Over two hundred thousand Aztecs died."

"It still seems amazing that Cortés with such a small group could take over an entire country," you say.

"It is," Manuel says. "Of course, an epidemic of smallpox caught from the invaders did almost as much to end the Indian civilization. The country was rebuilt on the European model with the Spanish as the slave masters of those Mexican people who remained."

→ → → → → → → → → → → →

Go on to the next page.

For the next few weeks, you live in a small tent at the edge of the clearing and help Manuel and Sylvanus excavate the pyramid. It's exciting work, as the pyramid emerges from under layers and layers of soil and vegetation. Huge, grotesque—but also strangely beautiful—mythological creatures emerge, flanking the stairway. Traces of color—reds, oranges, and blues—still cling to parts of the carvings.

You become so interested that when Sylvanus leaves for a short trip to the States, you stay with Manuel to help in the search for other pyramids nearby.

It looks like it will be a long time before you return home to New Jersey. And for the time being, you don't mind at all.

The End

"If it's all right with you, then, I'll head back to school," you say.

"We'll go together," John Reed says. "I have a wagon already waiting at the edge of camp. We'll be in El Paso tomorrow. There, we'll get a train going north."

"You remind me of someone I knew in Egypt," you say, as the two of you head toward the border. "His name is T. E. Lawrence."

"Lawrence?" Reed says. "That name sounds familiar. I remember now, we've been getting reports at the paper about a Lawrence in Arabia. Is your friend any relation?"

"That's him," you say. "So you've heard about him? Is he all right?"

"As far as I know he is," Reed says. "He seems to be helping organize the Arabs to fight with the British against the Turks. You've really been around, I see. You'd make a good reporter. After you finish school, maybe you'd like to try your hand at it."

"I'm not sure *what* I'm going to do," you say.

"Exciting things are happening all over the world, and you and I will both be part of them," Reed says. "I have a feeling that our paths will cross again one day."

Reed is right, you think. There are many things to do in the world. And it's hard to know in which direction to go. First, you'll have to get back and finish school. Then you have the rest of your life to decide.

The End

You decide to go back home with Frank. Pershing sees to it that you get seats on the afternoon train going north.

"We never did get to see Mexico," you say, looking out the window as the countryside rolls by.

"Maybe we'll get down there after graduation," Frank says.

"Maybe," you say.

The End

You decide to go with the troopers.

"I'm an American, and I need to get back to school. Can I go with you?" you ask the captain.

"Sure," he says. "Fall in line behind the column. When we are out of this sector, I'll have someone guide you to safety."

As you jump on your horse, you call to Remy, "Your real fight is across the ocean, you know. Come on, let's get out of here!"

Remy stands there for a moment trying to decide. Then he jumps on his horse and comes over beside you.

"*Ah, mon ami, vous avez raison.* You are right. I must help drive the invaders from my *own* country," Remy says.

Later, at a temporary supply base not far from Ciudad Guerrero, you learn that the Villistas have been driven off, and Villa himself is either killed or seriously wounded. Strangely, you feel sad.

The next day, you and Remy follow the hospital wagons carrying the wounded to El Paso. From there, you both get a train going north.

You haven't decided yet, but you have a feeling that when Remy returns to his homeland, you may be going with him.

The End

Glossary

Adobe—An unfired brick of clay or earth that has been dried in the sun. Widely used in the southwest United States and in Mexico for building houses and other structures.

Aztecs—Fierce, warlike people that dominated central Mexico at the time of the Spanish conquest. The Aztec empire was overthrown by Hernán Cortés and a small band of Spanish adventurers. This was accomplished with the backing of thousands of Indian allies who were eager to revolt against the harsh Aztec rule.

Cantina—A combined saloon, restaurant, and general store. Cantinas often provided entertainment as well.

Carranza, Venustiano (1859–1920)—A leader in the Mexican civil war, he overthrew the dictatorship of Díaz. Carranza became the first president of the new Mexican republic. Though more liberal than Díaz, he dragged his feet on social reform and was opposed by both Pancho Villa and Zapata. His forces finally defeated those of Villa and Zapata, but he himself was assassinated.

Díaz, José de la Cruz Porfirio (1830–1915)—When the French withdrew from the military occupation of Mexico in 1867, Díaz established himself as president and ruled with an iron hand for thirty-five years. He was finally overthrown by a revolution led by Madero.

Frijoles—Beans, usually fried and served as a kind of paste. A staple food of Mexico.

Hearst, William Randolph (1863–1951)—A newspaper publisher and creator of the "yellow press," a combination of glaring headlines and sensational stories. Hearst owned a chain of newspapers that served virtually every part of the United States. One of the richest men in the world, he owned vast estates around the globe, including in Mexico.

Huerta, Victoriano (1854–1916)—Graduated from the Mexican Military Academy in 1875 and became a brigadier general. Madero sent Huerta to suppress the different peasant uprisings that had broken out across the country. Later, Huerta took over the government himself and ruled as a military dictator. After a dispute with the United States led to an American attack on Veracruz, Huerta abdicated and fled Mexico.

Juárez, Benito Pablo (1806–1872)—Born of Indian parents in the Mexican state of Oaxaca, Juárez became president of Mexico in 1857. His government, however, went bankrupt. Because of the debts owed to France, that country militarily took over Mexico and installed Maximilian (1832–1867) as "emperor." In 1867, the French were forced out and Maximilian executed. Juárez was again elected president, after which he instituted many liberal reforms.

Madero, Francisco (1873–1913)—A liberal Mexican leader, Madero was educated at the University of California and in Europe. A firm believer in democracy, he opposed the dictatorship of Díaz. He called upon the Mexican people to rebel, which they did, electing Madero president in 1911. Madero was later betrayed by his own army commander, Huerta, who had him assassinated.

Maximilian (1832–1867)—An archduke of Austria, Maximilian was set up as emperor of Mexico by the military forces of the French emperor Napoleon III. Though he upheld many of the reforms of Juárez, his government lacked popular support and relied solely on the French army of occupation. When the United States finally forced a French withdrawal, Maximilian was executed by the Mexicans.

Patton, George Smith, Jr. (1885–1945)—A graduate of the U.S. Military Academy in 1909, Patton served with General Pershing in Mexico, in particular in the chase after Pancho Villa. Patton later accompanied Pershing to France in 1917. There, Patton showed an intense interest in the tank, a "secret weapon" just introduced by the British. Between World War I and World War II, Patton continued to argue the value of the tank. He was nicknamed "Old Blood and Guts" by his men.

Pershing, John Joseph (1860–1948)—A graduate of West Point, Pershing served with the cavalry in the campaign against the Apaches in the southwestern United States and northern Mexico. Promoted to captain, he was later jumped from captain to brigadier general by President Theodore Roosevelt against the protests of seniority-minded officers. In 1913 he was sent to the Mexican border in command of a cavalry brigade, and in 1916 he pursued the Mexican revolutionary Pancho Villa into Mexico. Later, he was the commander of the American Expeditionary Force sent to France in 1917.

Reed, John (1887–1920)—An American reporter for the New York papers *The World* and *Met-*

ropolitan, as well as the author of many books and magazine articles. A close friend of Pancho Villa, he wrote a book, *Insurgent Mexico*, about his experiences with this leader. Later he wrote *Ten Days That Shook the World* about his on-the-scene reporting of the Russian Revolution.

Sombrero—A broad-rimmed hat of felt worn originally in Spain and then adopted as a popular form of dress in Mexico.

Tortilla—A thin, flat, unleavened loaf of corn or wheat bread, baked in an oven.

Villa, born Doreteo Arango (1878–1923)—Later took the name of Francisco Villa and was nicknamed "Pancho" by his followers. He was the son of a laborer and orphaned at an early age. When he was still very young, he killed the owner of the estate on which he worked for assaulting his sister. He then fled to the mountains and spent his adolescence as a bandit. He had no formal education but taught himself to read and write and had a lifelong respect for learning. He was caught and sent to prison but escaped and went to the U.S. Later, he returned to Mexico and recruited several thousand men to fight against the Mexican government, which he considered corrupt. When the fighting was finally settled, he was given a pardon but was assassinated three years later.

Wilson, Woodrow (1856–1924)—An author and educator, Wilson became president of Princeton University, governor of New Jersey, and later president of the United States. Sensing America's coming involvement in the war in Europe, he did not want a war with Mexico in 1916. His main concern was to protect American interests by supporting the status quo of the Mexican government.

Zapata, Emiliano (1883–1919)—An Indian like Juárez, Zapata worked as a stableman on a hacienda before becoming a soldier in a cavalry regiment. Later he began a rebellion of landless Indians and was for a while an ally of Villa, during which time they teamed up to occupy Mexico City. Neither their occupation of Mexico City nor their partnership lasted very long. Although allies against the government, they never found a real basis of cooperation. Zapata fought the government until he was killed in an ambush.

Suggested Reading

If you enjoyed this book, here are some other books on Mexico that you might like:

Alba, Victor. *The Horizon Concise History of Mexico*. New York: American Heritage Publishing Co., Inc., 1973. A very readable history, with many black and white illustrations and a few color plates. Like the *Time-Life* books, it is one of a series and strives to give an overview of the history of each country covered.

Editors of Time-Life Books. *Mexico*. Amsterdam: Time-Life Books, 1958. One of the *Time-Life* "Library of Nations" books, this is a collection of heavily illustrated articles on the history and culture of Mexico. It is more of a full-color picture-essay with text.

Haas, Antonio. *Mexico*. New York: Scala Books, 1982. A giant, glossy, deluxe book with many full-page photos. The text traces the history of Mexico from the Olmec Indians, the creators of the "mother culture" of Mexico, to the present. It emphasizes the grandeur and variety of Mexican culture.

Innes, Hammond. *The Conquistadors*. New York: Alfred A. Knopf, 1969. This book tells the story of the conquest of Mexico by a handful of Spanish soldiers of fortune led by Hernán Cortés. It also includes a smaller section on the conquest of Peru by a similar group led by Francisco Pizarro. Both are told in a clear style with many illustrations and forty-eight pages of color plates.

Riding, Alan. *Distant Neighbors*. New York: Alfred A. Knopf, 1985. An in-depth examination of Mexican history, decade by decade, with an emphasis on the character of the Mexicans and the often difficult relations between the United States and Mexico—"a land at once familiar and exotically foreign."

Tompkins, Peter. *Mysteries of the Mexican Pyramids*. New York: Harper & Row, 1976. This is the companion book to the author's Egyptian book, *Secrets of the Great Pyramids*. It details many wild theories about the Mexican pyramids (reputed to have been built by survivors of "Atlantis," for example) but also contains much solid material.

ABOUT THE AUTHOR

RICHARD BRIGHTFIELD is a graduate of Johns Hopkins University, where he studied biology, psychology, and archaeology. For many years he worked as a graphic designer at Columbia University. He has written many books in the Choose Your Own Adventure series, including *Master of Kung Fu*, *Master of Tae Kwon Do*, *Hijacked!*, and *Master of Karate*. In addition, Mr. Brightfield is the author of *The Valley of the Kings*, the first book in The Young Indiana Jones Chronicles series. He has also coauthored more than a dozen game books with his wife, Glory. The Brightfields and their daughter, Savitri, now live on the coast of southern Florida.

ABOUT THE ILLUSTRATOR

FRANK BOLLE studied at Pratt Institute. He has worked as an illustrator for many national magazines and now creates and draws cartoons for magazines as well. He has also worked in advertising and children's educational materials and has drawn and collaborated on several newspaper comic strips, including *Annie* and *Winnie Winkle*. He has illustrated many books in the Choose Your Own Adventure series, most recently *The Lost Ninja*, *Daredevil Park*, *Kidnapped!*, *The Terrorist Trap*, *Ghost Train*, and *Magic Monster*. He is also the illustrator of *The Valley of the Kings*, the first book in The Young Indiana Jones Chronicles series. A native of Brooklyn Heights, New York, Mr. Bolle now lives and works in Westport, Connecticut.